I0572611

Hanna's Blessings
We Pray, Pray, Pray Series

Written by: Carline Constant and Gregory Constant
Illustrated by: Leena Shariq

Subtitle: Grateful For God's Many Blessings.

For information contact us online at: www.sprinklejoybooks.com

Summary:

Hanna's Blessings takes us on a journey of faith with Hanna and her grandmother. Together, they celebrate the true meaning of Christmas. Grandma encourages Hanna to participate in the value of giving to others and being grateful For God's blessings.

Subjects:
CYAC: 1. Christmas Story Grateful For God's Blessings-Realistic Fiction Book. 2. Faith Based Grandparent Grandchildren's Book Religious Christianity Realistic Fiction Book. 3. Godly Morals & Values-Prayerbook Family Realistic Children's Book. 4. Kids-Picture Book. 5. Kids Spiritual Life Lessons-Christianity. 6. Raising Spiritual Kids-Praying Habits-Christian Picture Book. 7. Christian Message Book. 8. Pray With Hanna Grandma & Caleb Christian Series-With Christian-Activities. 9. Christian Message Picture Book. 10. African American Christian Family-Realistic Fiction.

Identifiers:
Paperback ISBN # 979-8-9921558-0-8
Hardcover ISBN # 979-8-9921558-1-5
ebook ISBN # 979-8-9921558-0-8

Library of Congress Control Number: 2024925918.

All scripture quotations marked (GNT) are from the Good News Bible Translation in Today's English Version-Copyright © 1993 by American Bible Society. Used by permission.

Printed in the United States of America
LCCN Imprint: Sprinkle Joy Publishing, New York.

10 9 8 7 6 5 4 3 2 1
First Edition: December 2024

Semi Realistic Art Style
For Ages 5-12

This book is a work of fiction, a product of the authors' imagination. Any similarities, references to characters, names, places, events, real people (living or dead), or real places are coincidental.

FOLLOWING LYRICS & MELODY IN PUBLIC DOMAIN - ORIGINAL COMPOSERS OF MUSIC:
1. "Adeste Fideles", "Come, All Ye Faithful", by John Francis Wade 1735-1740.
2. "Away in a Manger", by James Murray stanzas in 1887.
3. "Joy to the World", by Isaac Watts 1674-1748.
4. "We Wish You a Merry Christmas", unknown, 1500.
5. "Silent Night", by Joseph Mohr in 1816 and Franz Xaver Gruber in 1818.

Sprinkle Joy Publishing Books

 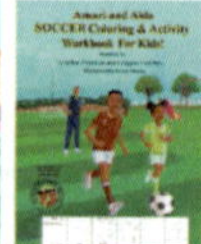     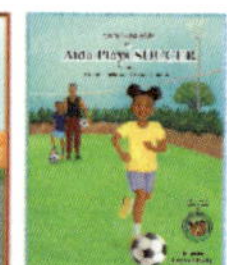  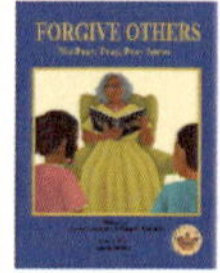  

www.sprinklejoybooks.com

THIS BOOK
BELONGS TO:

____

WITH GRATEFUL HEARTS TO GOD!

To God be the glory!

****

This book is dedicated to my three sons, Gregory, Anthony, and Andy.

May God continue to mold and shape the three of you into responsible men.

Thanks to my family and friends for your words of encouragement.

Thanks to the editors for your contributions.

To all children and families worldwide.

-Carline Constant

Thanks to God for the many blessings.

-Gregory Constant

Hanna's Blessings
We Pray, Pray, Pray Series

Written by

Carline Constant and **Gregory Constant**

Illustrated by **Leena Shariq**

It's the morning of Christmas Eve.
Sweet melodies ring throughout our church.
I sing along, "COME, ALL YE FAITHFUL,
JOYFUL AND TRIUMPHANT…"

"COME,
ALL YE FAITHFUL,

JOYFUL
AND
TRIUMPHANT..."

When the song ends, Grandma gently kneels beside me.
She softly prays, "God, I love You with all my heart.
I have faith in You, my God.
Thank You, God, for Christmas and
Your many blessings."
I close my eyes and say a prayer, too.

"God, thanks for my many Christmas gifts."
Grandma smiles down at me.
"Hanna, it's exciting to receive
presents, but Christmas is about
sharing God's blessings
and having a grateful heart."
"Grandma, what are God's
blessings?" I ask.

"We are grateful for God's many blessings in our lives, like good health, family, a joyful heart, food, clothing, a warm home, friends and much more," Grandma says.

"Hanna, we celebrate God giving us His Son,
Jesus Christ, on Christmas Day.
A blessing to the whole world.
Through the year, we continue to receive God's
blessings and His kind gifts. On Christmas,
God teaches us that it is better that we give
gifts than to receive them.
The Bible says that God loves the one
who gives gladly."

"Is that why we celebrate Christmas with presents—
to give gifts to others Grandma?"
"I like when I receive presents.
Why is it better to give them?"

Grandma chuckles and says, "Sweetie, when we give
to others with a grateful heart, we share the blessings
God has given to us."
*I wonder what I can do to share the blessings that
God has given me.*
Grandma and I head home singing,
"AWAY IN A MANGER, NO CRIB FOR A BED,
THE LITTLE LORD JESUS LAID DOWN HIS
SWEET HEAD..."

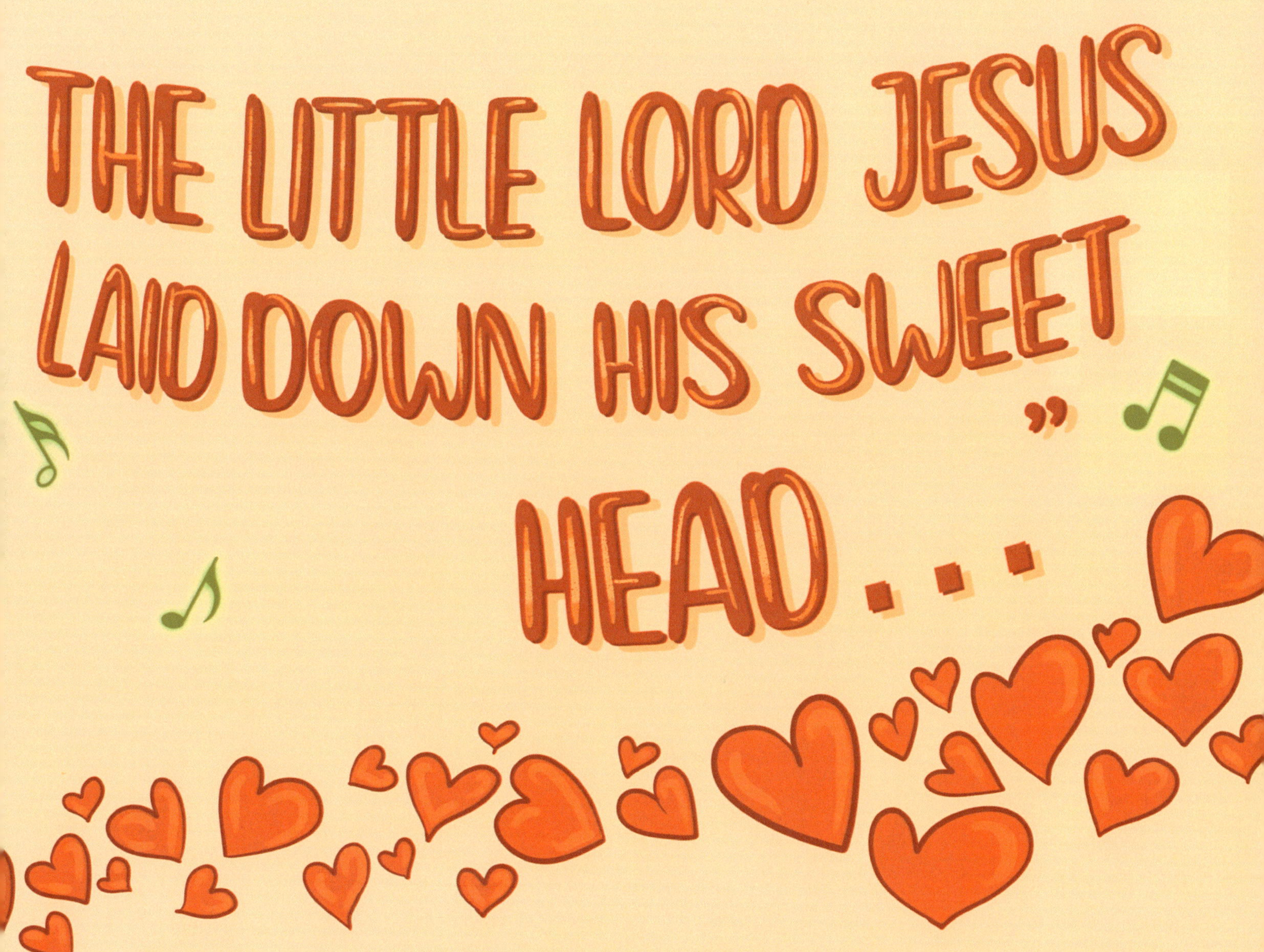

Later, our family gathers to go out caroling
on this special night.
Grandma's big smile makes me smile.
Together we sing, "JOY TO THE WORLD THE LORD
IS COME, LET EARTH RECEIVE HER KING…"

We come to a home at the end of the street where new neighbors recently moved in. There are no lights hanging or any decorations outside.
A woman opens the door, she also chants along with us, "WE WISH YOU A MERRY CHRISTMAS…"
I notice a girl peeking out from behind the woman.
She looks sad and she's not singing.
I smile and wave to her.
Grandma welcomes the family to the neighborhood and hands them a basket.

"Thank you for the songs and this wonderful welcome gift," the woman says with a grin.
I greet the girl. "Hello. I'm Hanna. What's your name?"
"Hi, I'm Cathy," she mutters quickly and looks away.
Why is she so sad? Tomorrow is Christmas!
I think to myself.
Maybe there's something I can do to cheer her up.

Cathy's Mom invites us in to share the cookies we gave to her.
I follow Cathy inside and I am shocked to see her house is nearly empty.
There aren't any stockings on the wall.
There isn't even a Christmas tree in sight.
Where do they put the presents?
Could Cathy perhaps not have any presents, either?

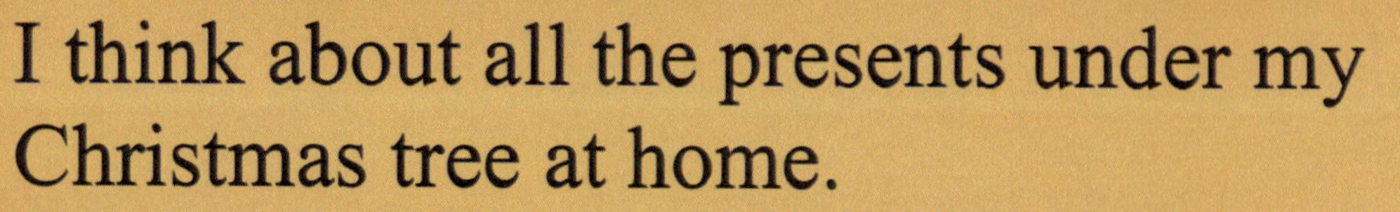

I think about all the presents under my
Christmas tree at home.
God blesses me with so many presents,
but I can share them.
Maybe I can give some of them to Cathy.
I whisper to Grandma,
"I figured out a way that I can share my blessings.

I want to give Cathy some of my Christmas presents."
"Sweetie, that's so generous," Grandma replies.
"Her family is going through a difficult time."

Grandma talks to Cathy's mother, to see if it is okay and she agrees. Grandma and I walk back home. Quickly, we change labels on the fancy boxes of presents. I grab my little Christmas tree before Grandma, and I head out the door.

Returning to Cathy's house, we surprise her with my gifts.
"Merry Christmas!" Grandma and I shout with glee. Cathy smiles, joyfully.
"Wow! I wasn't expecting any gifts this Christmas. Thank you!"
Her mother and Grandma help arrange the small Christmas tree in their living room.
Cathy and I organize the gifts.

Cathy looks at me and says, "But, I don't have a gift to give you, Hanna."
"That's okay," I tell her.
"Christmas is about sharing God's blessings. These are my gifts to you and making a new friend is your gift to me. Merry Christmas, Cathy!"

Heading back to church, Grandma and I sing,
"SILENT NIGHT, HOLY NIGHT!
ALL IS CALM, ALL IS BRIGHT…"

I kneel and pray,
"God, I'm grateful for Your blessings,
a loving family, my new friend,
and a warm home.
I thank You, God, for helping me
to be a blessing! Merry Christmas!"

Love God.
Love Your Neighbors.
Jesus is the Reason for the Season
★ BELIEVE ★

MERRY CHRISTMAS

God, thank You for the gift of Jesus.

✝ **Bible Verses:**

"Out of the fullness of his grace he has blessed us all, giving us one blessing after another."
(John 1:16 GNT)

"For it is by God's grace that you have been saved through faith. It is not the result of your own efforts, but God's gift, so that no one can boast about it."
(Ephesians 2:8-9 GNT)

"For God loves the one who gives gladly."
(2 Corinthians 7-8 GNT)

"This hope does not disappoint us, for God has poured out his love into our hearts by means of the Holy Spirit, who is God's gift to us."
(Romans 5:5 GNT)

GOD, THANKS FOR THE BLESSINGS!

Directions: Write a letter to thank God. Remember to write your name on the first line. <u>Next, write about who you can share Jesus Christ with and pray for this Christmas</u>, be sure to explain why. Color the gift boxes.

Date:________________

Dear God,

It's _______________________________. I love You! God, one blessing I thank You for is *family* because _______________________________________.

God, the second blessing I thank You for is ____________________because

____.

God, the third blessing I thank You for is ____________________because

____.

★★★

Who can you share Jesus Christ with and pray for this Christmas?

God, this Christmas, I want to share Christ with and pray for________________

____

BLESSINGS WORD SEARCH

Directions: Find and circle the following hidden words.

BLESSINGS	SHARING	PRAYER
~~FAITH~~	CHRISTMAS	VALUE
KINDNESS	JESUS	

P	F	D	W	F	F	Q	D	J	E	Y	V
N	S	E	U	L	A	V	R	P	A	G	H
W	Y	K	E	P	I	U	C	X	N	U	F
Y	R	I	F	B	T	H	H	I	C	O	J
Q	Z	N	T	X	H	C	R	P	I	O	I
U	R	D	O	I	T	A	I	R	M	G	S
R	S	N	T	R	H	H	S	A	A	P	T
B	V	E	Q	S	Q	Z	T	Y	M	N	D
H	P	S	Q	C	S	F	M	E	X	C	W
J	E	S	U	S	T	S	A	R	K	C	C
G	V	K	S	G	N	I	S	S	E	L	B
U	G	K	Q	B	H	E	P	P	P	S	O

"My heart praises the Lord; my soul is glad because of God my Savior."
(Luke 1:46-47 GNT)

BLESSINGS

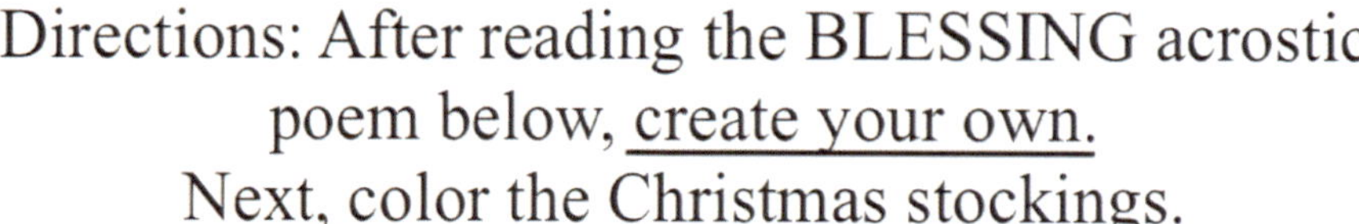

Directions: After reading the BLESSING acrostic poem below, <u>create your own.</u>
Next, color the Christmas stockings.

BLESSING

B - Be generous and kind.

L - Love one another.

E - Each person needs to pray to God.

S - Show your love to one another.

S - Share Jesus Christ with others.

I - In God, we have Faith.

N - Need God's grace and mercy,

G - God is love.

BLESSING

B - _______________________________

L - _______________________________

E - _______________________________

S - _______________________________

S - _______________________________

I - _______________________________

N - _______________________________

G - _______________________________

WORDS TO KNOW

Blessing	Something good in our lives that comes from God.
Christmas	Celebrating the birth of Jesus Christ.
Christmas Eve	The day or evening before Christmas Day.
Faith	Confidence in God.
Jesus Christ	Son of God given to us on Christmas.
Kindness	To be caring and helpful to others.
Prayer	Talking and listening to God.
Sharing	Giving up something you have to someone else.
Values	Beliefs based on Biblical values.

About the Authors:

Carline Constant and Gregory Constant are a mother and son duo dedicated to spreading positivity through literature. They hope Sprinkle Joy Publishing books touch the hearts and minds of people everywhere. Each sentence, illustration and story telling idea of Sprinkle Joy Publishing books are made with love!

Carline Constant is a mother, author, and educator. She earned a Master's Degree in Education from Brooklyn College City University of New York.

Gregory Constant is an author, entrepreneur, and technology professional. He earned a Bachelor's Degree in Informatics from the State University of New York at Albany.

For information about Sprinkle Joy Publishing Books contact us online at:
www.sprinklejoybooks.com

About the Illustrator:

Leena Shariq is a self-taught, Pakistan-based children's book Illustrator and Portrait Artist. Always encouraged by her parents, Leena started freelancing at the age of 16, and now, after only four years, she has illustrated many children's books, one after another.
Her body of work consists of semi realistic illustrations and stylised portraiture.

 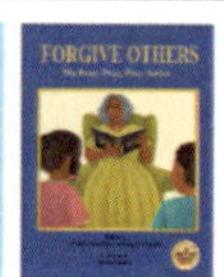   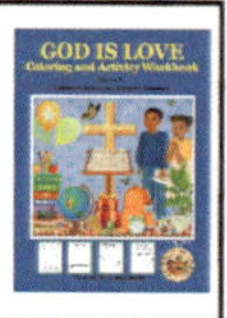  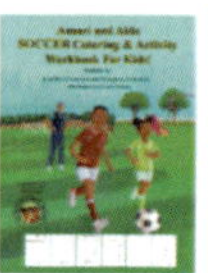     

(We Pray With Hanna, Grandma, & Caleb Series)
I AM THANKFUL
FORGIVE OTHERS
BE THANKFUL: Pray at Mealtime
Hanna's Blessings
GOD IS LOVE Coloring and Activity Workbook

Also, by Sprinkle Joy Publishing Books
(Aida and Amari Series):
The Champ
Amari and Aida SOCCER Coloring and Activity Workbook for Kids!
Aida's Joy
Aida's First Day of School.
Amari Plays Basketball.
Amari and Aida in HOW TO PLAY BASKETBALL.
Aida Plays SOCCER. (coming soon)
Amari's Helping Hands (coming soon)
Amari and Aida in FUN TIME Coloring & Activity WORKBOOK For Kids!
Thanks to God for ALL!

Thank you for your purchase!
Please leave an honest review. We read every review
and they help new readers discover our books.

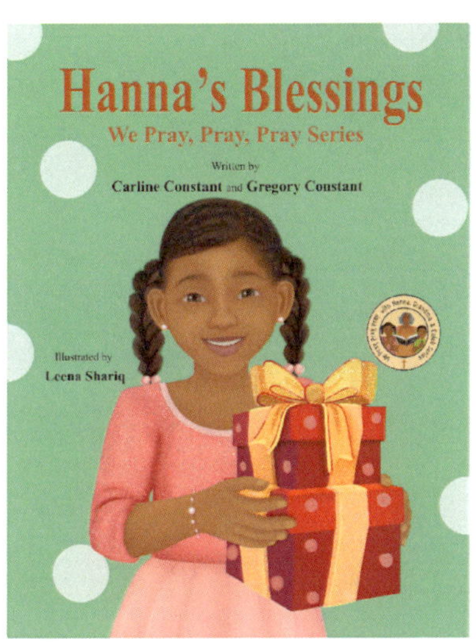

Order Sprinkle Joy Publishing Books
www.sprinklejoybooks.com

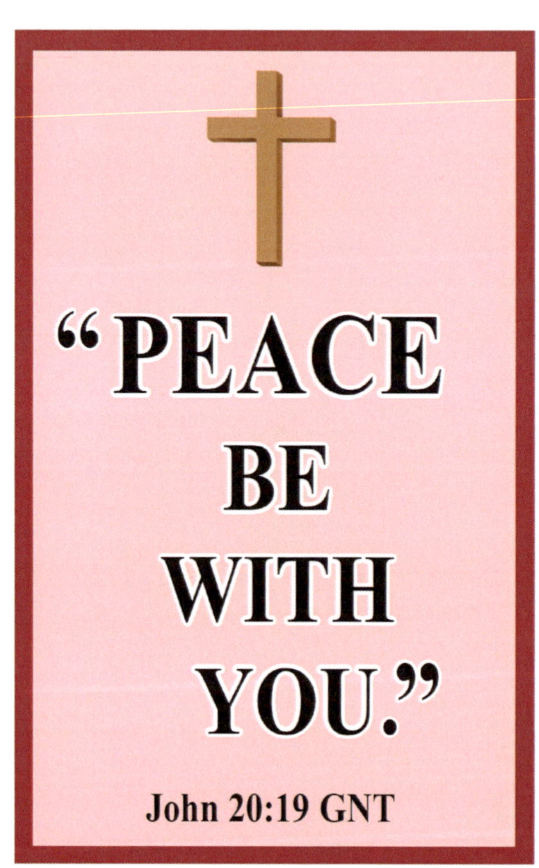
"PEACE
BE
WITH
YOU."
John 20:19 GNT